Ukrainian Fairy Tales

Illustrations of Y. Vasnetsov, M. Rudachenko, E. Rachev

Translated by Victor Voloshchuk

The three popular Ukrainian fairy tales about animals are presented in this book. The Ukrainian children love these fairy tales very much, and I hope that their peers around the world will love it too.

The rooster and two little mice

There were two little mice named Twister and Twirler, and a rooster Sonorous Throat. The little mice did not do anything just danced and sang. And the rooster got up in the morning, woke everyone with his song and set to work.

Once the rooster was sweeping in the courtyard and found the ear of wheat.

"Hey! Twister! Twirler!" called the rooster. "Look here what I have found!"

The little mice came and said:

"It would be good to thresh this..."

"And who will do it?" asked the rooster.

"Don't me!" replied the first little mouse.

"Don't me!" said the second one.

"I will do," said the rooster and began to work.

And the little mice continued to play.

The rooster threshed the ear of wheat and shouted again:

"Hey Twister, hey Twirler, come and see how many grains I have got!"

The little mice came.

"It is necessary," they said, "to bring grains to the mill and to grind the flour."

"And who will do it?" asked the rooster.

"Don't me!" said Twister.

"Don't me!" shouted Twirler.

"Well, I'll do it," said the rooster. He took the bag onto his shoulders and left.

And the little mice continued to play. When the rooster came home, he called again the little mice:

"Hey! Twister! Hey! Twirler! I brought the flour."

The little mice came and rejoiced:

"Oh! Dear rooster! Now it wants to knead the dough and bake the pies!"

"Who will do it?" asked the rooster.

"Don't me!" squeaked Twister.

"Don't me!" screamed Twirler.

The rooster thought and said:

"I'll have to do it, probably."

After kneading dough, he brought wood and heated the oven. Then he put in it the pies.

Meanwhile, the little mice continued to sing and dance.

Finally, the pies were baked. The rooster took it out of the oven and put on the table. The little mouse immediately rushed to the table, not even waiting to be called.

 "Oh, I'm hungry!" said Twister.

"And I'm hungry too!" give a cry Twirler. And they sat at the table.

Then the rooster said:

"Wait a bit! First, tell me please who found the ear of wheat?"

"You have done," the little mice shouted.

"And who thrashed it?"

"Also you did," more quietly uttered Twister and Twirler.

"And who had kneaded the dough, heated the oven and baked the pies?"

"You did," yet more quietly told the little mouse.

"And what have you did?"

What could say in reply the little mouse? Nothing at all! They started to get out from the table, and the rooster did not hold them. Who is going to treat with the pies such sluggards?

The hare's hut

In a large forest there were a fox and a hare. Each of them had a hut. The fox's hut was made from ice, and the hare's one was made from wood.

When the spring came, the fox's hut melted away.
And the hare's hut continued standing on a hill.

The fox decided to trick the hare. She asked to sleep
one night in his hut, and then drove him away!

The hare was walking along the road, crying. And suddenly he saw two dogs:

"Bowwow! Why are you crying, hare?"

And he replied:

"How can I not cry? I had a wood hut and the fox had an ice one. Spring had come; the fox's hut was melted. She asked me to spend the one night in mine, and then she kicked me out!"

"Don't cry, hare! We will help you in your trouble!"

They all three came to the hut and the dogs barked:

"Bowwow! Run away, brazen fox!"

And the fox answered from the hut:

"As I will jump out, your fur would fly to all corners!"

The dogs were frightened and ran away.

The hare walked along the road again, tears rolled down his cheeks. Next the bear met him:

"Why, hare, are you crying?"

"How can I, bear, not cry? I had a wood hut and the fox had an ice one. Spring had come, the fox's hut was melted. She asked me to spend the one night in mine, and then she kicked me out!"

"Don't cry, hare! I will help in your calamity!"

They both approached the hut and the bear roared:

"Go, impudent fox, away!"

And the fox shouted from the hut:

"As I will jump out, your fur would fly to all corners!"

The bear frightened and fled into the forest.

The hare went along the road again, and bitter tears streamed from his eyes. But soon he met a rooster with a scythe:

"Doodle-do! Why are you crying, hare?"

"How can I, rooster, not cry? I had a wood hut and the fox had an ice one. Spring had come, the fox hut was melted. She asked me to spend the one night in mine, and then she kicked me out!"

"Don't cry, hare, I'll drive her out."

"No, rooster, you cannot do it! The two dogs have tried, but they were frightened and ran away. The bear also was trying, but unsuccessfully. So you are unlikely to be able to master the fox..."

"Let's go, and you would see what should happen!"

They approached the hut, and the rooster stomped with his boots, flapped with his wings and cried:

"Doodle-do! I go through the forests and mountains in boots with spurs. I have a scythe on my shoulder! Flee, fox, from the hut!"

The fox was frightened and said:

"I'm already putting shoes on!"

And the rooster gave a cry again:

"Doodle-do! I have a scythe on my shoulder! I want to chop you in pieces! Flee, fox, away!"

The fox said again:

"I am already dressing!"

The rooster shouted for the third time:

"Doodle-do! I have a scythe on my shoulder! I want to cut your head out! Flee, fox, away!"

Then the fox jumped out from the house and gasping ran into the forest.

And the hare became living in his hut again.

The mitten

An old man accompanied by a dog walked through the forest. And he accidentally dropped his mitten.

A mouse ran up, got into the mitten and said:

"I will live here!"

Before long, a frog galloped and asked:

"Who is in this cottage?"

"I am Mouse-rodent. And who are you?"

"I'm Frog-chatterer. Let me go in!"

Now, two residents were in the mitten. A hare ran past; he saw the mitten and asked:

"Who is in this habitation?"

"Here are Mouse-rodent and Frog-chatterer. And who are you?"

"My name is Hare-runner. Let me go in!"

"Come in!"

There were three of them already.

A fox ran along the path, and she also noticed the mitten:

"Who are living in this lodging?"

"Here are Mouse-rodent, Frog-chatterer and Hare-runner. And who are you?"

"I am Fox-sister. Let me go in!"

"Come in!"

There were four of them already. Next a wolf approached the mitten and asked:

"Who lives in this compartment?"

"Here are Mouse-rodent, Frog-chatterer, Hare-
runner and Fox-sister. And who are you?"

"I'm Wolf-brother. Let me go in!"

"Come in!"

He also got into the mitten. There were five of them
already.

A bit later, a wild boar came.

"Oink! Oink! Oink! And who lives in these quarters?"

"Here are Mouse-rodent, Frog-chatterer, Hare-runner, Fox-sister and Wolf-brother. And who are you?"

"Oink! Oink! Oink! I'm Boar-fang. Let me go in!"

"It is a trouble! Who is passing by, everyone wants to get in! But here is closely without you."

"I will try to enter. Please let me go in!"

"What to do with you, come in!"

The wild boar crept into the mitten too. The six of them were within already. And it was now as closely as in a barrel of herrings.

Suddenly, the bushes crackled and a bear got out of it and roared:

"Who are dwelling in this shack?"

"Here are Mouse-rodent, Frog-chatterer, Hare-runner, Fox-sister, Wolf-brother and Boar-fang. And who are you?"

"Oho! How many of you are here! And I'm Bear-roamer. Let me go in too!"

"Where will we let you go, when it's so tight already?"

"But I will try to find room somehow."

"Let it be so, come in!"

The bear got in; after that there were the seven of them already.

Meanwhile, the old man felt that his hands were cold; he began to look for mittens and found that one of them was missing. Then he went back, and a dog was running in front of him. Soon the dog saw that the mitten was lying on the ground and moving. The dog barked: "Woof! Woof! Woof!"

All inhabitants of the mitten were very scared; they jumped out and scattered themselves around the forest.

The old man came and took his mitten.